George Brinley Evans was born in Dyffryn Cellwen in 1925. He began work in Banwen Colliery, aged 14 in 1939. He joined the army at 18 and served in Burma with the 856 Motor Boats, first with the 15th Indian Corps then the 12th Army. He returned to Banwen colliery after the war, married Peggy Jones and raised a family before losing an eye in an accident in the Cornish Drift. He began to produce work as a sculptor in addition to his painting after his accident and also wrote scripts for independent television and the BBC. He returned to industry and finally to opencast mining in 1977. His fiction, painting and sculptures have been widely published and exhibited. He still lives and works in Banwen.

PARTHIAN BOOKS

BOYS OF GOLD

George Brinley Evans

PARTHIAN BOOKS

Parthian Books
53 Colum Road
Cardiff
CF10 3EF
www.parthianbooks.co.uk

First published in 2000.
All rights reserved.
© George Brinley Evans
ISBN 1-902638-12-3

Reprinted in 2001

Typeset in Galliard by NW.

Printed and bound by ColourBooks, Dublin, Ireland.

The publishers would like to thank the Arts Council of
Wales for support in the publication of this volume.

With support from the Parthian Collective.

Cover: Coggin Four Feet by George Brinley Evans
emulsion & water-colour on paper

A CIP catalogue record for this book is available from
the British Library.

To Peggy,

and for

Noel, Emily, Jamie and Naomi.

With thanks to Sue Owen and her girls at the DOVE for solving

the Banwen enigma. And to Carol Anne (Evans) Williams for

typing my first script back in 1962.

And to Eira for time and patience.

Stories

'It depended on the soldier and how he bore himself.'

Text from *The Campaign in Burma*, H.M. Stationery Office 1946.

BOYS OF GOLD

The steamer was a small, thirty year old, coal burning cargo/passenger boat, that until Pearl Harbour had plied her trade quietly between the ports on the shores of the Bay of Bengal. Now with a number in place of a name, painted fleet grey, she was steaming as part of a battle group.

He had been brought back from Akyab with the rest; a week in Calcutta and Captain Belton had asked for volunteers. Two trucks took them to a hot empty plain, miles from anywhere, just seven tents set alongside a sparkling river. Most of the next day was spent swimming, until the medics arrived, along with the ammunition. It was jabs all round.

The evening was spent charging Bren magazines with ball, tracer and incendiary bullets. The following morning they were aboard ship, on their way. Two days out, under the bluest of blue skies, they were ordered to check their kit. They had handed their pay books to the Q.M. before embarking. He had handed them proxy forms, for the coming parliamentary elections, back home. Not one of them had been old enough to sign. Belton's kindergarten, someone mocked. He felt for his dog tags; they were there, one red, one black, strung on his army issue cord necklace. Thomas Samuel. 11741178. C. of E. The armourer at Brecon had punched on the information. He had stopped thinking of himself as a Samuel. Now, when people called his name, he automatically answered to Taff. He sat down on the deck next to Bagley, closed his eyes and listened to the rhythmic slap-slap of the bow wave; not long now.

* * * * * * * *

The afon Pyrddin gleamed and shimmered as it slid over the smooth stones, swirled, spun, and turned, then bent itself over the Sgwd Fach, the first of its three waterfalls. On and over, headlong down the one hundred foot drop of the Horseshoe Falls, into a dark, dank gorge, filled with the sound of angry, hissing water, breaking and splitting itself into a grey boiling mist; only to fall back into the iron grip of the millstone grit. Raging in its narrow channel, it rushed for the freedom of the smooth, wide shelf above the Lady Falls, to billow out like clouds of white silk, into the sun-filled pool below.

What a wonderful place for a body to live, he thought. He looked over Mrs Strong's garden to Ianto the Farm's big field. It shone a warm buttercup yellow in the morning sun. Almost in the centre stood a nursery, a stand of some thirty to forty full-grown Scots firs. A hideaway place that could turn into a steaming jungle, if you wanted it to. Where every shadow was an envelope for some new terror and so frightening, warned Billy Whitticker, "It would give you lock-jaw right enough! Right!"

Or if you held your head on one side and looked through the cobweb of your eyelashes, it would become a desert fort. Standing in the long shadow of an Arabian sunset, with white capped legionnaires standing sentinel. Once it was the Metz Wood they had read about in *The Wizard*. They had become the heroic, defiant men of the Welch regiment. Up from their young souls had surged the craving of an ancient inherited valour; through their milk white teeth they had cried the cry, "Stick it the Welsh!" and they had meant it.

"Sammy! Sammy! Sa...mmy!" His mother's voice sang out. He hated people calling him Sammy, except his mother, and that best of all when they two were alone together. He liked everyone else to call him just plain Sam.

"Come on then, if you're going with Owen to pick whinberries. Sit in your place." He looked at his brother, two years

10

older than himself, who said without malice, "won't wait for you mind, if you can't keep up."

"Mammy! Owen's going to leave Sammy on the mountain," his sister piped up. She was sat in their father's chair, still in her nightdress; her hair tied up in rag curlers. She was the youngest and only girl, so could do and say what she liked.

"If they only dare!" his mother had said. The clean scent of her skin close to him, a wisp of her hair brushed his cheek and a small voice inside him whispered, "I love you, and I'll bring you back more whinberries than anybody's ever seen."

She gave him one of his father's old tommy-boxes, burnished to a bright pewter by the emery rough hands of a collier. To Owen she gave the Christmas biscuit tin and the bottle with the home-made pop. They bought the ginger pop off a girl called Dolly, who brought it around, on a Friday, in a handcart, that ran on an old set of pram wheels and bore on its sides the words "Polar Ajax Explosive", from the days when it was a box that carried gelignite to the colliery.

Alan was ready and came around.

"You mind Sammy, now!" their mother called after them.

The sound of her voice made Mr Gay, the Frenchman who lived opposite, lift his head from the storm of colour that was his flower garden. The tough old peasant from the Ardennes raised his hand in greeting to the boys.

"Good morning, Mr Gay!" they shouted back respectfully. He was the only foreigner they knew and hadn't he shown them the merry-go-round he had made for his grandson, with its painted, prancing horse?

"Takes a Frenchman to make something like that," Alan had said.

"And where are you away to, Sam?"

"Hello, Mrs Strong," he smiled at the kind eyes that looked down on him. "Going to pick whinberries, I am," he announced his impending venture to the tall figure leaning against the gate. "I'll bring you some if you like," realising that perhaps he had found a way of repaying the soft-spoken lady for all the sprigs of mint she'd passed over the fence to little Mrs Thomas, as she called his mother, every time they had lamb for dinner. And every St. David's Day since he had started school she'd brought him the best leek in her garden, the one with the greenest leaves and the whitest root, to pin on his coat; and one for Owen.

Mrs Strong laughed. Her life had begun in a small village outside Whitehaven that stood right in the way of the North Atlantic wind as it came in like ice off the Solway Firth and took its spite out on the half a dozen cottages that some insolent Cumberland miners had built right in its path. She accepted and forgave his extravagances with the natural compassion bred into those born in such places.

When they reached the bridge by the Pant, Rafferty was waiting for them.

"Got money for your permits? MacDermitt the shepherd is up by the Bwthin," warned Rafferty.

He felt in his pocket for the silver thrupence his mother had given him. MacDermitt lived alone in a small valley hidden high on Mynydd Cefn Hir, tending a flock of sheep and guarding that part of the estate that belonged to the Williams family of Aberpergwm. He had only ever seen MacDermitt once, when the man had been making his monthly trip down to the village to shop. The memory of him came flooding back, as he lengthened his stride to keep up with the others. How could such a small pony carry such a big man? He was as wide as a piano.

They went down over the quoit pitch and behind Hopkins' shop. He looked across the colliery horse's field to Banwen colliery, the world's biggest anthracite mine. Owned by David Martin Evans Bevan, one thousand, two hundred men worked there. His father was one and he would be another.

"Do you know how MacDermitt do disbaddy young rams?" Rafferty was asking "Just tips them up and bites their balls off!" Liar, he thought. But winced all the same.

The Bwthin was nothing more than a ruin. When David

Thomas, a fireman at Banwen colliery, lived there with his family, it was called Ty-yr-heol (The Road House), for this was no ordinary road. The road they walked on was Sarn Helen, built on the orders of the Emperor Maximus and the road, it was said, along which St. Patrick was led to slavery by Irish raiders, from his home at Banwen.

This time the raider was a massive Scot, sat on a pile of stones. And although the sun had already made the stones warm to the touch, MacDermitt was wearing a heavy tweed shepherd's coat, a tweed hat, leggings and half-sprung boots. The hair that showed from under his hat was snow white, as were his bushy eyebrows and the stubble of his moustache and beard. His eyes were light blue and clear like a boy's and shone out over the weather-raw skin that covered his cheekbones.

"Can my brother and me pick on the same permit, Mister?" asked Owen.

"No. One picker, one permit, laddie."

He gave his brother his thrupence. Owen handed over the sixpence. "Thrupence each," Owen said.

"What do you call the wee boy?"

He stepped out from behind Owen to show himself. MacDermitt smiled at him. At the sight of those long tobacco-stained teeth, he stepped back, and was sorry he had thought Rafferty a liar.

The second part of the climb up Cefn Hir was steep and could only be made on hands and knees. Owen kept looking back at him; he was sorry he was making Owen feel guilty. But the wind-burnt grass was making the bottoms of his boots shine and chafing the skin between his fingers.

"Not much further now, Sam," Owen encouraged from a little higher up. The tone of his voice regretting the earlier hard looks.

Alan got to the wall first, and was standing on top of it. They had reached the top of the mountain. Owen held out his hand.

"Come on, Sam. The Roman Wall!" He scorned the helping hand and ran on to the wall. The wall stretched for as far as the eye could see, along the top-most ridge of the mountain, held together by nothing more than the builder's ability to balance one stone on top of another.

"Get up on it, Sam!" his brother urged. "Take a look."

It was like looking over the edge of the world. Below him lay MacDermitt's domain. The beautiful landlocked valley of Blaen Pergwm. Its shape reminded him of the fans the girls had carried in the school play, "Princess Chrysanthemum". Tucked down, hundreds of feet below, MacDermitt's cottage was the thumb that drew the centre folds together. The lovely golden fabric of the fan rippled like a summer sea, as the tall mountain grass bent its head to the soft breeze. Dotted out like painted flowers were the pickers, their heads bowed and deft fingers urgently plucking the ripe fruit from its stalk.

"Come on, mark your name on the wall," shouted Rafferty. Alan had already finished scraping his name through the powder-dry moss. It was as well; two summers away lurked the consumption.

"You have a rest, Sam. I'll do your name for you," offered Owen. "Samuel Thomas 1932", Owen finished off his name and the date neatly. He was glad Owen was his brother.

"No good picking on top by here, better go down a bit," organised Rafferty.

When they reached the first group of pickers, Owen warned, "Mind where you're putting your feet now, in case you step into one of their baskets."

Mrs Morgan and her children made up the first group, all picking into helpers, old tea cups, that when full were tipped into two fourteen pound wicker baskets. The whinberries, still in their powdered bloom, lay like a purple cushion against the shining brown wicker walls. If there was such a thing as professional whinberry pickers in Banwen, then this family was it. When a basket would become full, one of the children would take it down the mountain and give it to Shurry, the bus conductor. At Neath he would give the basket to the man who kept the centre stall at the market.

Four or five pence a pound, Mrs Morgan got for her whinberries. A full day's work brought them in seven or eight shillings, if they were lucky. They found a place to pick, but only after religiously observing the laws of "Bara-y-cwtch". This was a custom that designated territorial rights to the picker already on the spot. The size of the allotment was nowhere stated but usually the bigger and more ferocious the picker on the spot was, the larger the area of his preserve became.

There were whinberries everywhere; how he wished he had brought two of his father's old tommy-boxes, or a bigger tin. The first whinberry he picked burst between his fingers. Never mind, he thought, there's plenty more. The next one dropped into a tangle of stalks and leaves. Then the insects, that until then had been busy feeding on the long grass, found him. They buzzed their inquiries around his head, in his hair, into his ears and nostrils, along his bare legs and down his shirtfront. The others picked diligently, insects or no insects.

"Alright, Sam?" Owen called.

"Yes, alright." He looked down at the few badly mauled whinberries that rattled around the bottom of the tin. And about two hours later, he could have done without Rafferty announcing to the world, "Hey! Look lads, poor old Sammy hasn't covered the bottom of his tin yet."

They stopped to eat. Owen gave him the sandwiches from the bottom of the pack, because they had stayed the freshest. But not even the banana sandwiches and the ginger pop improved his efficiency. Then it was time to go home. The bottom of his tommy-box was covered by about two inches of whinberries, no more; and that included squashed whinberries, red whinberries, not to mention the bits of grass and pieces of stalk.

The pledges he had so readily made weighed on him. His feet dragged themselves through the bracken, not wanting to carry him to where he would have to confess that those pledges would not be kept. In the evening light, he was frightened by the massiveness of the mountain's dark curves. He would never come after whinberries again, never. Nor would he, he was going to think, ever come on this ugly mountain again, but stopped himself, thinking that perhaps he'd better wait until he got home first.

At the side of the house, Owen took the lid of his tin: "Tip yours in here, Sam."

He opened his tin and looked at the jammy mess.

"Go on. Never mind, tip 'em in, Sam."

Their father was in the back yard, legging a mandrill. He looked up and smiled, "How's it going, Owen-Sam?"

He grinned back at the smiling man and the fear of the mountain flew from him.

The table was laid for supper, and the kitchen full of the smell of newly-pressed linen their mother was folding on to the airer.

"Well then?" She stood there, with a snow-white pillow slip over her hands, like a muff.

Owen lifted the lid of his tin; the Christmas biscuit tin was full to within an inch from the top.

"Sam and me managed this much between us, Mam." He looked at Owen; Owen was looking at their mother, looking at her eyes. Looking for what only a son can see in the eyes of his mother. And no man ever born has seen it in any other place. In that instant of light, you bask, you bathe; you become the boy of pure gold.

* * * * * * * *

"Come on, Taff, move!"

The bump against the jetty brought him to his feet. He

waited to follow Bagley up the rope ladder. The loop he had made in the cotton bandolier slipped. He fastened it to the "D" buckle of his pack and shinned up the ladder after Bagley. Bagley bent to help him over the edge of the jetty. He saw it coming through the air towards him. For a moment, he thought it was a bundle of rags. Until it thumped down heavily on the deck in front of him. The mouth wide open, showing strong white teeth bloodstained from having almost bitten the tongue in half. He rose to his feet and his eyes met the eyes of the Indian sepoy, who had booted the head at them. The sepoy stopped grinning.

"Taffy!" Bagley's voice was a mixture of impatience and concern, something the young Englishman often felt at his comrade's seemingly unending ability to wander into trouble. They ran across the jetty, over the road and jumped through the window of a bank. They landed up to the tops of their boots in money. They picked it up by the armful, useless paper money. They kicked it around.

"Bagley! Thomas!" They ran out into the street to where the captain's shout had come from and formed into Indian file with the rest. Now they had to make their way through the city to the main railway station. He looked down and let the worthless paper money, still in his hand, slip through his fingers. And thought of the death head, the matted blood-soaked hair a mother had once washed and gently brushed into curls. The eyes, so full of the terror of death, a father had looked into to see the reflection of his own dream. Of the torn and bruised lips, pressing and receiving loving kisses.

The sun blazed down, turning the green of their shirts to black with rivers of sweat and scattering the stench of death to every corner of this once shining city.

"Right! Everybody got one up the spout! And check your safety catches!" Sergeant Hopper's voice banged around the empty street.

The soft, gentle breath of a mountain breeze passed across his face, his feet were on mountain bracken and his mouth filled with the clean, clean scent of his mother. He stepped off along the road behind Bagley.

Thirty yards away, crouched behind a pile of rubble that not long ago had been a shop of sorts, a twenty year old Japanese infantryman felt a pulse racing in his finger as he bent it around the trigger. Knowing the moment he pressed that trigger, his life would end in minutes. His strong, young body smashed to pulp in a hail of tracer, ball and incendiary bullets.

Carefully, he framed the face of the British soldier in the aperture of his rifle sight, felt the soft warmth of the palms of his mother's hands against his temples, sucked in a deep sigh and pressed the trigger.

ICONS

He handed in his tally and his lamp was banged down on to the counter of the lamp-room hatch.

"Pick up your butty's powder tin. He's had to go to the manager's office." The message was passed clearly and in a tone that warned against any temptation to back-chat.

He stood behind the others in the queue at the powder shed. He could taste the steam, in the clear morning air, as it leaked in spurts from the heavily lagged pipeline that fed the engine-house.

The sweet aroma of high explosives flowed out over the half-door, with the arm that handed him the long oval powder-tin. "Here, catch. Four hundred and seven's." The tin held twenty sticks, five pounds of Thames Polar Ajax gelignite.

A group of his pals waited for him near the mouth of the Drift.

"Leningrad's relieved."

"I know. Heard it on the wireless."

"Hey! What's them you're wearing?"

"What do they look like?"

The unyielding wooden soles felt strange under his feet. Leather was in short supply, a shoemaker at Neath had taken to making clogs, and they were coupon-free.

He put the Oxo tin that held his two precious Woodbine into a hole in the wall, along with the other makeshift cigarette cases.

At the locking station, the fireman searched him and tested his lamp.

"Your butty got any holes ready?"

"Yes. Three coal holes."

The fireman took three shining copper electric detonators from a small, sturdy leather pouch; the inside was divided into sections, like a honeycomb, to keep the ultra sensitive detonators apart.

"Here, put these in your pocket. Put them safe now! Tell him to ram the holes ready for me. I'm by myself, see."

"Right'o!"

"You make sure you tell him now!"

"I will. I will!"

"Less of your lip! And get off to your work!"

He reached their heading, hung his lamp on a nail that had been driven into a timber upright; on another, he hung his coat that had two large pockets, made of duck, sailcloth, sewn on by his mother. Handy, pockets; left your hands free for carrying and made it harder for the rats to get at your food.

He pulled the key of the tool-bar out of his waistcoat pocket. He had it tied to a bootlace, like a fob on a watch-chain, and one of the detonators came with it and fell to the floor. He picked it up, took the other two detonators out of his pocket and put all three on a ledge level with his eyes; stood the powder tin where no one would fall over it, slid the copper rammer off the tool-bar and walked onto the face.

Standing there was the reason for his butty's enforced visit to the manager's office. The last tram they had filled the day before had not been taken out.

His butty arrived, sweating and out of breath. "Afternoon shift haulier stopped the place. Horse roofing. Bloody idiot, brought Hector in here. That great camel of a horse. How daft can you get! Anyway, the night shift's put it right now."

Horses worked without light. When a horse pulling a tram, weighing perhaps two tons, collided at full speed with a section of low roof, the skin under the horse's collar would be burst open, causing the animal intense pain.

The dayshift haulier clattered in with an empty tram, unhitched the horse. The three of them lifted and tipped the empty tram off the track, to make way for the full tram to be taken out.

"Come back! Silver! Come back!"

The horse turned around to the left at the shouted

command, and backed up to the full tram to be hitched.

"Silver! Silver! Come on, lad! Silver!" The horse sprang forward, like an athlete off his mark. The tug chains cracked taut, the horse gasped as the collar brought the full weight of the loaded tram against its breast. The three of them pushed, to help the horse get the heavy tram moving from a standing start. "Silver! Silver! Come on, lad!" Slowly the tram eased away. "The fireman wants us to ram the holes ready."

"I know, I met him on the way down. Get the powder tin and the dets. And bring some clay for ramming."

He came back with the powder tin and detonators and dropped them onto the pyramid of coal dust, left by the drill, then threw down a ball of clay.

"That's all the clay there is!"

"Don't throw those dets about like that, you young clown! You trying to blow us all up ? Go back to the road and look for some horse shit. Roll that into plugs for ramming. And don't you be long about it!"

He smiled as he went back; he liked giving the crusty old bugger a start – brought him down a peg or two.

Seven full trams and a pair of timber later, he was sat with his father and brother at the dinner table: bathed, and his eyelashes smeared in Vaseline. His brother grinned at him, "He's started courting, Mam."

He felt his mother coil a strand of hair, from the crown of his head, around her finger and gently tug, "Well?"

His brother carried on gleefully, "It's Peggy. Marie the Paper's little sister!"

"I thought Peggy was still at school?"

He kept looking at his plate.

Another gentle tug, "You lost your tongue?"

"No."

"No what?"

"No, she's not still at school."

He had thought she was too, until that Sunday he had seen

her standing in the doorway of her mother's house. The last time he had seen her, she'd been just a bit of a kid.

The Vaseline ran in rivulets from the corners of his eyes, carrying the coal dust with it; he wiped it away and washed his face.

The crystal clear waters of the Afon Pyrddin sparkled in the sunlight, as they raced and tumbled over the smooth rocks.

He picked a flower from a cluster of Ragged Robins and gave it to her: "They call it Lychins fos-cuculi." He had heard it called that on the wireless, the day before.

She looked at the delicate red flower, with its narrow segmented petals, then at him and smiled, "Do they now?"

In his brain, in the centre of his forehead, he carried an icon of her, like that. Dark brown hair, almost black, flecked with auburn in the sun. She had the fair skin of a Celt, fair and without a blemish, and green, laughing eyes.

"I'm going to join the army!"

She put her hand on his and squeezed his fingers, "Stop showing off."

* * *

As he was being marched with the others from the railway station and in through the main gate of Brecon Barracks, he wondered, had he been showing off?

They were still laughing when Bob dropped the speed from full ahead to dead slow. It had been a terrible trick to play, but it was a chance that had come begging. They hadn't done it because the bloke was an officer. Somebody has got to be an officer. But this replacement for the old man, well, they really didn't know what to make of him. Like their old C.O., most of the lads were wartime volunteers and just couldn't fathom the guy. He actually did think of the locals as wogs.

They had been coming down river, three Japanese prisoners on board, and there was Mr Pomposity himself, on the river bank giving the semaphore call-up signal at a mile a minute, looking as if he was going to take off. So they waved back, the Japanese prisoners joining in, and sailed straight past. And from that distance they could see the replacement captain turning a bright puce.

Bob nosed the boat into an island of sampans and junks. When the forest of masts and washing hung out to dry was sufficient to hide them, they stopped. Having persuaded the Japanese – using sign language – to look after the boat, their guns and ammunition they gave them what was left of a tin of fifty Woodbine and then shot off to the newly opened Mayo Marine Club.

An afternoon of swimming in a deliciously clean pool, tea in china cups, sandwiches and cakes made by the ladies of the Anglo-Burmese W.V.S., then back to the boat, with two bottles of tea and a bag of rock-cakes for the Japanese prisoners.

It was slack water; they kept at half speed going back up stream. The mile-wide river, usually the colour of mud, was a mirror of shimmering pink in the evening light. Clouds of flying foxes lifted from the mangrove swamps that lined the riverbank, and flew into the advancing night.

The Japanese prisoners sat amidships; tea and cakes gone, and most of the Woodbine. They had been away from home four years and more, on active service, but prisoners of war for only two weeks.

He looked at the close-cropped head in front of him, staring out over the rose-pink river. A soldier on active service, in moments of quiet, is never very far from a daydream.

He wondered what image, what icon, that cropped head carried in the centre of its forehead? Perhaps the sweet breath of a girl as she turned her face up to be kissed?

Or the fragrance of his mother as she pressed him to her, the kind of mother that sewed oversized pockets on to working coats...

The rest of the boats had unloaded their prisoners. Three

Seven Three pulled alongside and unloaded. The Japanese were formed up, and were ready to be marched away. Their Lieutenant came up, saluted, "Those men," he pointed to the three back-markers, who were grinning and waving, one holding a Woodbine tin, "are asking, can they help to crew this boat again, tomorrow?"

"Sure. OK."

The replacement captain was watching, still seething. He glared at the two British soldiers, then at the three Japanese prisoners, then back at the two Britishers. Their stance was brazen; they had about them an air of insolence that was almost tangible. He wanted to act, he would act, but he'd let it go this time. The next time, they'd be for it. The Japanese were brought to attention, there was nothing in their bearing that hinted at their prisoner status, and were marched off. The three temporary crew members of Three Seven Three smartly brought up the rear.

SHIPS THAT PASS

They got to the Foundry jetty, which was as far as they were to go. They would sleep there that night in what, until the night before, had been a Jap billet and before that the manager's house. But only after they had got rid of the awful stench coming from a swollen, decomposing corpse, alive with maggots, outside one of the windows.

They found a tank of fuel oil. Soaked some sacking in it, and draped the oily shroud over the heaving corpse and cremated whoever it had been.

The following morning three of the boats were to leave for Bassein and contact the Royal Welch Fusiliers, who had fought their way there. Then they were to inquire after some French nuns who had run a school in the town. But first they had to fuel up at jetty number seven.

It was "D" day plus one. A submarine was tied alongside, its generators being used to provide electricity to the newly captured city of Rangoon. A dead man lay, as if lounging, near one of the sheds. He walked past.

It was then that he saw her for the first time, and her very appearance there, at that place and at that time, was startling.

Her small, perfectly shaped feet splashed in the monsoon rain, on the jetty's deck. Jet black hair, pulled up tight into a topknot, showed off the bloom on her lovely, cream-coloured skin. A small, beautifully moulded nose, each nostril bejewelled, and a mouth warm from smiling. Her slender body bowed, to support a basket of wares held against a protruding hip. She held her head, tilted, a little to one side, giving notice of her bubbling humour. Her eyes were almond shaped and liquid.

When they had not been skiving or chasing dacoits, they had all met her and bought her wares. At that same jetty, jetty number seven.

Eighteen months they had been soldiering in the Delta, a bog the size of Wales. Always hungry. At night, enveloped in the stifling humidity of the mangrove swamps. Frightened, drenched in sweat, straining to listen over the rush of noise set up by multitudes of insects and shoals of bloated, croaking frogs. Large, wet rats scurrying about in the darkness, their bold, darting, red eyes making your skin crawl. Other times if you were unlucky being smothered in red raw, weeping ringworm.

They had helped take one of the dacoit leaders. A lithe young man, naked but for a piece of rag he wore as a jockstrap. Spotless brown skin, black, spiky hair, bright, intelligent, dark eyes. When he'd been brought in, his arms had been pulled brutally behind him and pinioned by shining steel manacles. He was executed in public two months later. No one he knew went to watch the hanging.

He held out the gifts he had bought her, from the Naafi van that called at their lines: two bars of Kit Kat and a bar of Lux soap, "England jaiga!" he had announced.

Her beautiful eyes blinked once, she took the gifts and stuffed them under her tight, white bodice. From her basket she took a packet, rolled into the shape of a cone, made from an old newspaper, and gave it to him. "Peanuts, Sahib!" Her voice was light and gentle, like the morning breeze off the Irrawaddy. "No annas, Sahib!" As with her ilk, the world over, pride was everything.

He shook himself awake. Twelve of them had travelled to London crumpled up in a mini-bus. The tall, young sergeant, back ramrod straight, the breeze blowing the black ribbons of his glengarry against the side of his face, barked, "Right! Stop talking now!" Then very courteously, "Quiet now, gentlemen please! Number one column! Column! Column shun! Column! Column will move to the right in column of route! Right-turn!"

Number one column, made up of five hundred men from Wales and the West of England, turned to the right, a little shaky, on the shiny yellow gravel.

"Number one column! Column! By the right! Quick march! Right wheel!"

The skirl of pipes sounded out over Horse Guard's Parade, and un-crumpled the lads of number one column.

Through the arch, into Whitehall. The pavements were packed with people; cheering, flag-waving, smiling people. People it seemed from every corner of the earth. Then he remembered her. A small figure, standing, outlined against the mirrored surface of that great river, in a far away, harsh, beautiful land.

And wondered, if sometimes-she-ever-remembered-him-from-her-so-many-many-patrons? He struggled to get back into step. What-could-she-have-been? *Panch-barras*? Six ? Seven-years-old-at-most. Remember-him? She-was-everybody's-favourite-peanut-seller. Remember-you ? You-daft-old-bugger.

"Number one column! Column! Halt! Left turn! Right dress! Eyes front! Stand at ease! Stand easy!"

He looked up at the white clouds racing across the blue sky. How quick the time had gone.

THE END OF SUMMER

It was half past six in the morning, only six and a half hours into the New Year and bitterly cold. His mother pulled the collar of his overcoat tight about his neck; her lips brushed his cheek, "Be a good boy now."

Hywel breathed in her fresh scent.

His father and brother waited in the back yard.

"You got your water and your grub box?" his father shouted.

"Yes."

"Come on then, let your mother go in out of the cold!"

He followed his father and brother out of the yard.

Two weeks earlier in December 1939 Hywel had left Maesmarchog Elementary School with three of his friends. Will "Jammy" Owens, Glyndwr Hill, and Talwyn Gimblet. Talwyn was the eldest, fourteen years and ten weeks old.

This was to be their first day as collier boys at Maesmarchog Colliery. Twelve hundred men worked at Maesmarchog, Wales's biggest anthracite mine. The road to the colliery was packed with men and boys, all huddled against the biting cold. No one spoke, except for a brief "Shwmae!" or a "Duw, Duw! It's a bloody cold 'un!"

Their hobnailed boots struck out a staccato rhythm on the frost hard surface of the Sarn Helen. A rhythm Hywel felt that made him at one with generations of boys who had strode to manhood over the ancient Roman way.

The manager's office was full of overmen, firemen and gaffer-hauliers reporting on or off shift. The comforting unforgettable smell of Davey lamps burning, the urgent ringing of wall telephones being wound up. Men he had known as neighbours looked different, more authoritative.

Mr Bob Jones, sidesman at St David's church, not wearing his Lloyd-George collar, but the blue flannel shirt and dark crocheted tie, the badge of the South West Wales colliery official.

"Shwmae, Rees?" the overman greeted his father.

Mr Bob Jones looked down at him, his gaze steady. "Take him in to John. He'll give him his number and sign him on. And you, young man. You pay attention to what's going on around you. Right?"

"Right," he gulped, his mouth dry.

His father guided him by the shoulder into the chief-clerk's office.

"Your number is twelve twenty-seven, Hywel bach. Remember it now! Sign here where I've marked with a blacklead," John Lewis instructed.

He dipped the pen into the ink, then carefully tapped the nib against the rim of the inkwell and signed his name neatly, under W J Owens.

The colliery yard was crowded with horses being led by their hauliers. Powerful animals, standing between fifteen and sixteen hands and weighing anything from fourteen to eighteen or nineteen hundredweight. Bred in Ireland especially for the drift mines of South West Wales, out of breeds such as the Suffolk Punch, Percheron, and the heavy Cob. No place here for the proverbial pit pony. Each horse had a feed bag tied about its neck and wore a collar and bridle. The bridle was a sturdy leather mask covering the whole face, except for the eyes, nostrils and ears. They were stabled in the best of conditions, a stall measuring twelve feet by eight, fresh, clean bedding, a full manger of oilcake and new cut chaff every day. During a shift they could be hauling trams weighing two tons and more up from deeps, or shafting trams down from heading, with gradients so steep, the overwhelming weight would often bring them to their knees. They would be brought out to the surface to be brushed, curry combed and hosed down with warm water, piped from the boiler house. They shivered with pleasure as the water poured over their tired, aching limbs. Unled, they homed into their spotlessly-clean stalls, each with a nameplate – Ajax, Caesar, Hector, each a suitably brave name. Little wonder they pranced, arched their necks, held their heads in haughty arrogance and snorted steam into the cold morning air.

His brother had collected his own lamp and their father's powder tin and was standing near the lamproom hatch.

"Here's your powder tin. I'm off with Edgar," he handed the tin of gelignite to their father. "See you after," he winked and grinned at his brother before hurrying away to find Edgar.

"Let's get you a lamp then," his father dropped his lamp tally on to a pile of shining brass tallies. Everything about the lamproom shone. Rows of Davey lamps, their yellow flames burning evenly behind polished, sparkling glasses that reflected in metal burnished bright by work-hardened hands. Behind them, row upon row of electric hand lamps, with fully charged accumulators feeding their flat white lights. Some boys were still given oil lamps when they started work. From what he'd been told, he hoped he wouldn't be given one. The light would go out at the slightest bump. Then you'd have to walk back in the dark to the locking station, to get it relit. Or if you carried it on your belt, it got very hot, and the buttons of your flies became undone...

"It'll make your eyes water for sure!" his brother mocked.

"How's it going, Rees?" Wil Jones Lampman handed his father his lamp. "Now then, we got to find one for you, Hywel boy." Wil reached to the side and lifted an electric lamp off the shelf. "Let's have a look what we got by here," he twisted the top, to test the lock, then twisted the bottom to test the switch. "Here you are then, number four hundred and seven. Pick that tally up at the end of the shift. Right, Hywel ?"

A crowd of men stood around the mouth of the Drift, waiting for the horses to clear. The collier boys stood to one side, away from the men; one or two called out to him, his brother among them.

"You stay by here, for today! Give us your cigarettes," his father said quietly. He handed the Oxo tin containing two

Woodbines to his father, who put it with his own cigarette tin into a hole in the retaining wall.

The lamp was heavy, much heavier than an oil lamp, no wonder they called them bombies, and there was more than two miles to walk. They were searched and had their lamps tested.

For the first five hundred yards it was level going and dry underfoot. Then the roof disappeared into a nothingness, the ground, wet and slippery, fell away to an incline so steep he'd had to put his hand on the sides to steady himself. It was a fearful place.

Three hundred million years before, the earth's crust had been ripped apart by massive earthquakes. Nowhere more than in the anthracite coalfield, causing great faults that sometimes threw the coalseams hundreds of feet down; this was such a one.

The rock beds stood vertical and water poured down everywhere, water that stank of rotten eggs. The huge timbers reached up into the darkness, reminding him of the arcading he had seen in the great cathedral on his last school outing.

They turned left into a tunnel. There were lights in front of them, bobbing about: caplamps, only hauliers wore caplamps. The air became warm with the smell of horses. This was the double-parting, the marshalling yard, where the journeys – trains of trams – were made up. He heard a sound like none he had ever heard before, an awful gulping. A horse pulling a loaded tram into the parting, its breath coming in strangulated gasps, as it plunged against the massive weight pulling on its collar. Head low, swinging from side to side, mouth dripping, body fully distended, belly almost touching the ground, expanding and contracting like a bellows. Swerving to pull at an angle, to shunt the tram up to the journey, it cracked its fetlock against the rail. The tram banged into the journey, the horse strained with all its might to hold, nostrils flaring, gasping for breath.

"Good boy!" the haulier encouraged, stuck a wooden sprag into one of the wheels and pushed himself between the trams, to unhitch the horse and shackle the tram to the journey. "Back a bit good boy! Back a bit!"

Out on to the main deep of the four feet seam was a tunnel, lined with steel and timber, almost a mile long. Armoured power cable draped from one steel arch to another, supplying transformers that buzzed softly. The first level to the left was blocked off by an air-door, the braddice cloth nailed to the bottom of the door flapping noisily in the current of air that whistled under the door, short circuiting into the fandrift. The steel arches gave way to timber, French timber, pine, with thick red bark. Resin oozed from the notches cut into the crossbeams, forced out by the constant downward pressure from the roof, and brought with it the fragrance of the forest.

His father turned right, through a braddice curtain, into their level and hooked his finger on a roadnail that had been driven into an upright. "Hang your things by here."

A rat froze at his foot, then scurried away. He hung his top coat on the roadnail, then his small coat, once his school blazer; now with the customary two large pockets sewn on the inside. One to hold his bottle of water, the other his tommy-box.

"What's the curtain for?"

"To keep the air going down the main. Here, take hold of this." His father unlocked the toolbar and handed him a sledgehammer, taking a mandrill for himself. "Right, let's take a look at it, then."

He had tried to imagine what a coalface would look like: the amount of colour surprised him. The shining grey, marble-like roof. And the way the absolute blackness of the void from which the coal had been taken, the gob, contrasted with the pale hue of the barkless Norwegian spruce faceposts. These were held fast between the floor and roof by white, fresh-cut wooden wedges. The coal, glass hard, reflected their lamplights like a wall of tiny mirrors.

"We'll bore a top-hole, that's going to be our first job," his father tapped the roof with the head of the mandrill, which rang hard like a bell.

They carried the boring machine on to the face. His father opened out the heavy, square telescopic stand to its full height and stood it upright, flipping the handle of the threaded spindle on the top of the stand. It spun and tightened against the roof, keeping the stand in its place.

"Pass me the worm. That threaded bar!" The worm in place, ratchet handle fitted to one end, drill chuck to the other, they were ready to bore. His father hung his shirt on the side; the blue flannel cummerbund he wore next to his skin accentuated the power of his strong, lean body. The cummerbund was a habit many men his age had picked up when serving as infantrymen in the Great War. His father took sight from the worm to the rock face with the mandrill, and began to hack a notch for the drill to bite. The force of the blows sent stones flying everywhere and impelled air through his father's clenched teeth.

He was seeing this quiet, soft-spoken man in a new light, and it frightened him a bit.

"Pass me the short drill, there's a good boy."

The old easy tone in the voice chased away the fright.

The drill was fitted into the chuck and turned until it was tight against the rock.

"You stand top side, put your hands between mine. I pull, you push." His schoolboy hands were small, like a girl's, between his father's large fists.

His father set his feet, "Right!" and pulled the handle towards him. The drill squealed and screeched its way into the rock. He pushed with all his might, the soft skin on the palms of his hands folded and pinched against the iron handle. The ratchet played a small tune as the handle freewheeled back. Slowly, half a turn at a time, the drill screamed its way into the rock. Once or twice he lost the stroke and got pulled back but his father didn't seem to notice; he had the swing of an oarsman.

First drill out, four-foot drill in, a swig of water, another half-hour of pulling and pushing, and the bore-hole was complete.

"You alright, Hywel?" his father was drenched in sweat.

"Yes," he puffed, "but my hands are burning."

"When you want to pee, pee on 'em. It'll sting a bit mind, but then it'll be ok!"

They dismantled the drill-stand and carried it back to the tool-bar. His father unlocked the powder tin. Took out six sticks of gelignite and the place filled with the smell of pineapple.

"Don't you ever rub your hands in your face if you handle this stuff, mind! Bring on some of that clay and roll it into plugs for ramming."

"How many?"

"'Bout half a dozen."

Danny Shot pushed through the braddice curtain; he was loaded with the tools of his trade, copper ram rod, leather detonator bags, safety lamp, roll of yellow cable and a battery firing box.

"Ready for me, Rees? Hello, Hywel!" he laughed. "Tophole first day, hey! Never mind, better luck tomorrow."

"We'll give it six, Dan. That should do it," his father handed the shot-firer a stick of gelignite.

Danny thrust a brass marlin spike into the gelignite, took a shining detonator from a leather bag, unwound its long fuse wires and pushed the detonator into the hole he had made in the explosive. He placed the stick of explosive into the mouth of the bore-hole, detonator end in first. Pushed it to the back of the hole with the copper ramrod, allowing the long fuse wires to trail through his fingers. His father fed in the remainder, Danny ramrodded them home, then the clay plugs, letting just six inches of the detonator fuse wire hang from the mouth of the bore-hole.

Danny lifted his Davey lamp to the roof and tested for gas: it was clear. He started off back to the outby, paying out cable as he went, through the braddice curtains, then came back and started preparing the hitch to the bore-hole. His father put his shirt back on. "You go back with Danny, I'll go up through the face and stop anyone coming down!" He ducked into the face and was gone.

"Right, let's get back then!" Danny led the way through the tarred curtains. "Get in by here!" He turned into a tumbling place. "You face the side now!" Suddenly his voice was stern. He picked up his battery box, hitched the cables, fitted the brass firing handle, yelled at the top of his voice, "Fire!" and turned the handle.

The sudden violent crash of the explosion engulfed him, his ears popped and his mouth was forced open. For a moment he was stunned.

The braddice curtains flapped loudly. Clouds of thick white, bitter tasting smoke billowed around them.

His father came around from the top level. "Alright, Dan?"

"Sounded good, Rees," he laughed. "Made old Hywel by here jump a bit." Danny put a hand on his shoulder and patted him affectionately. "Never mind, first day's a bit of a shock for everybody, Hywel bach. Know what they told my old father on the day he started work? And that was more than sixty years ago! "Mae yr haf, bachgen di wedi pasio.—Your summer, boy, it is over." Danny Shot laughed as he translated.

He looked towards his father, who he knew was watching him, through the thick, swirling, white smoke.

THE FOURTH DEVICE

The three men sized-up their place of work. The deputy, Will Stephens, had not exaggerated. It was a bloody mess! A real bloody mess!

Water streamed from the shattered roof. Twisted steel arches hung down, their connecting fish-plates burst open. In the probing shafts of white light they looked grotesque, like the beaks of dead birds.

When the coal seams were laid down, eternally impervious nature also laid down a thin skim of mud between each band of rock. Clay joints, that when wet became a lubricant able to slide a mountain down into the valley in the blink of an eye.

The beams from their lamps reflected in the black pond of water that stretched off into the darkness of the inby.

"We won't wait for Gwyn. Post through the middle, steady it first," suggested Rees. Tom and Eric agreed.

Rees knelt down, put one hand on a fish-plate, its inch diameter bolts sheared clean off, pushed his other hand under the water and began scraping away loose debris.

"Pass me something to measure with." Tom handed him the sledgehammer. Taking it, he stood the hammer in the hole he had made, the head of the hammer reaching to about eight inches off the fish-plate. He put his hand, palm open, thumb outstretched, on top of the hammer, then handed the hammer back to Tom, "This! Six inches and a three finger lid!"

They worked quickly and quietly, hardly ever speaking, and were cautiously tightening the seventh post when they became aware of a massive weight beginning to move, right above their heads.

"Quiet!" breathed Eric.

Staying perfectly still, they listened.

"Christ! There's someone coming!" Tom shouted in disbelief. "I bet it's that bloody Gwyn!"

"Get back! Go back! Get to hell out of it!" they yelled

frantically. But the light came bouncing on towards them.

There was a tearing sound of rock beds being ripped like calico, a noise as if the earth was being torn apart. Timbers squealed and snapped, with reports as startling as gunfire. They threw themselves against the sides, into the water, anything to take what cover they could.

Slowly the turmoil died away, and the ground settled.

"Tom! Eric!" Rees shouted.

"I'm alright. What about Eric?" Tom pushed himself up.

"OK! I'm OK!" gasped Eric. He unclipped his lamp and sent the beam probing towards the outby. "Now who do you say that silly twat was?"

"Gwyn Jones. He's the only one with any business on here," Tom gasped, still breathless from fright.

Droplets of water sparkled like showers of diamonds as they fell through the beam of light.

They crawled through the pond, to the outby, careful not to brush or bump against anything. Huge slabs of shining, wet rock blocked their way. They were locked in.

"There!" yelled Tom. His lamplight picked out what looked like a half-submerged head.

Eric scrambled through the water. "Gimme a hand! Quick! Quick!" Eric, the youngest and strongest, heaved the top half of the unconscious Gwyn out of the water and began dragging him towards the small mound in front of the fall. "He's out cold. Pull his legs out of the water. Let's have a look at him."

Slowly and gently they examined the still unconscious Gwyn. They found no bleeding and his limbs seemed not to be broken.

Rees put the flat of his hand on Gwyn's throat. "Plenty of pulse." He pinched Gwyn's nose. "Gwyn! Gwyn! Gwyn!" Not a move.

"Get him comfortable. Bugger about, and we could make things worse," said Eric.

"Aye!" Tom agreed. "And let's have a look to see how the fuck we can get out!"

Their lamp beams swept the chamber. It was about four yards wide, ten or twelve in length, and in height, less than four feet from the shattered roof to a floor that was flooding with water. The noise of the rushing water surrounded them as they sat on a slab of rock.

"Put his head on your lap, Rees. Tom, try rubbing his legs to keep his body heat up. I'll go and have a look-see. You never know, could be lucky," said Eric, and set off through the water to the outby.

"You be careful now!" cautioned Rees. "One out for count is enough."

"I'll just look to the topside; looks like a bit of a hole." Eric sent the beam of his lamp prodding to the left corner. "See it?"

"Aye, but don't take chances," said Tom. "Rees is right. Will Stephens should be doing his rounds in a bit. He'll see the fall and get help."

"OK, OK. Just looking! You just keep trying to get Gwyn around," muttered Eric as he squeezed into the gap.

"Well?" shouted Tom.

"Well, bugger all," came Eric's muffled reply.

Eric crawled back to the mound. "Shift up. Still not a move yet?"

"He's breathing – light but steady," said Rees.

"Better than him struggling. He can't be in pain. He wouldn't just lay like this, would he?" asked Tom.

"No. You got a point there, Tom," Rees said.

"One thing we don't have to worry about," said Eric.

"We'd be buggered if he was in pain or bleeding – we got bugger all for him," grumbled Tom.

"Look – you keep his head on your lap, Rees. I'll lift his middle onto my lap – and you, Tom, take his feet. We'll huddle together – keep warm, right," said Eric.

"I think we'd better turn our lamps off, save the batteries.

I'll keep mine on dim," Rees said.

"Bugger all worth looking at anyway – pity we haven't got a piano," Tom grinned.

Full of apprehension, wet through and cold, Rees and Eric laughed at Tom's lopsided humour.

* * * * *

The only sound in the underground chamber, a mile into the mountain, was the dripping of water and the steady breathing of the men. The only light, a faint glow from Rees's lamp, still switched to dim. He had fallen into a disturbed sleep and woke with a violent start.

"Christ!" rasped Tom. "What's up?"

"Sorry! Sorry! Me dreaming, that's all," Rees blew into his cupped hands.

"You all right, now?" muttered Eric, arms wrapped tightly around himself.

"Aye! Dreamt we wasn't here!" Rees shivered. "Bugger waking up like that! Like waking up from a fit!" he shuddered and eased Gwyn's head on his lap.

"You'll give us all bloody fits – keep that up! growled Tom.

"My fucking legs are dead," groaned Eric. He switched on his lamp, hoping its bright, white light would somehow lessen the awful numbness of the black, wet cold, and was transfixed. "The water! The water! Look! It's gone!"

The three lamp beams skitted around, flitting off the wet rock. Water still dripped everywhere, but the pond had gone and the rail track was in sight.

"They've got a hole through!" shouted Tom. "We should hear something!"

"Quiet then! Let's listen," said Eric.

Huddled together, staying perfectly still, they listened. Nothing.

"Eric – you're the youngest – give 'em a tap on the rail –

get a bit of life back in your legs. The sledgehammer's by there, behind you," laughed Tom.

Eric eased Gwyn's legs off his lap, groaning as he straightened out his legs. "God almighty! I'll never walk proper again!" He found the hammer, crawled to the rail and hammered out a steady beat that rang out sharp and clear.

They listened. Nothing. Eric tried again. They listened, but again nothing.

Tom shone his light to the other side of the track. "Less droppers over by there, Eric – let's make a tidy place to sit."

Tom and Eric set about tipping stones off their sides and laying them flat. Tom found a strand of shiny detonator fuse wire, rolled it up into a ball, "Waste not, want not", and put it in his shirt pocket.

Eric put a length of broken timber across the back of the rough stone platform.

"Let's get Gwyn over by here." Eric crawled back to the mound. "Me and you, Rees, take his head and shoulders – and Tom, take his legs."

Very slowly they lifted the unconscious Gwyn and started to edge their way towards the rough-made couch.

"Careful now – careful!" gasped Rees. Gwyn was heavy.

The sharp stones dug into their knees and scraped their shins. Another yard and they had Gwyn on the stone couch.

"Bugger that for a game of soldiers!" puffed Tom.

Eric put the tips of his fingers against Gwyn's throat. "His pulse is there – but he's as cold as ice. Let's get back and huddle up to keep our heat." They lifted Gwyn back up onto their laps and pressed close to each other. "Wonder what made Gwyn late again tonight – M.C. at the Workingmen's I expect," grinned Eric.

"More than likely!" said Tom. "As long as he's around the ladies, he's right. It got him a few good thumpings in his younger days. Didn't it, Rees?"

"Aye – reached his pain-free zone now, I expect," grinned Rees. "At his age – it's divorcees and widows, appreciation instead of thumpings."

"Sh! Sh!... Quiet!" Eric lifted his hand and looked at the others for confirmation.

There was no need to ask, they could all hear it. It was unmistakable – faint, but unmistakable: the sound of men working.

They slapped each other on the back, hugged each other, shook hands, the awful torment of being trapped, the numbing cold for a moment forgotten. "We're on our way! Give 'em a knock, Eric!" Tom shouted.

Eric didn't need asking twice. He lifted Gwyn's legs off his lap, grabbed the sledgehammer and struck the rail. The steel rail rang like a bell. He stopped, they listened. No answer, but still the sound of men working.

"Try again, Eric – but this time try the one the kids use. Tom-tiddly-har-rah-brown-bread!" said Rees.

Eric hammered out the age old schoolboy's signal: it rang clear, vibrating along the steel rail. Once, twice, three times. Not moving a muscle, they listened. Nothing, just the faint sound of men working.

Eric hammered out the signal again, then again. They listened. There was the sound, faint rhythmic hammering. A sound they imagined. A sound they heard.

"Answer 'em! Answer 'em, er!" yelled Tom.

Eric hammered out an acknowledgement. They listened. There was the same faint sound of pulsating hammering.

"Right! Right! Let them get on with their work!" laughed Rees.

"Another once! Come on!" Tom was full of it. "Three times for a Welshman."

Eric happily obliged. They listened, again, to the distant, faint hammering.

"That's a sound to put you off bloody collieries for life!" growled Tom. Eric crawled back into the huddle to keep warm. A thin haze hung about them. Their wet clothes draining off what little body heat they had left.

"Wonder what time it is?" muttered Rees.

"Hometime! And the sooner the better for old Gwyn by here," said Tom.

"Hospital for him – more like. Must be mid-morning," guessed Eric.

"As long as there's not too many about – when we get out. That'll do me!" said Rees, suddenly very serious.

"Why?" asked Eric.

"Let's just say it'll suit me better," said Rees.

"Go on, bloody tell him! Soft bugger's on a hobble." said Tom in disgust.

"Bloody hell!" exclaimed Eric in disbelief. Rees, like Tom, was twenty years older than Eric. They were both top class craftsmen, before Thatcher, but very different kinds of men. Eric considered Rees to be part of the bedrock of old style unionism; miners' welfare, libraries, internationalism, in some things more rigid than a nonconformist deacon. And now to be told he was on the fiddle. He looked away.

"It's a long story, Eric. If I had been able to sell the house I wouldn't have wanted the hobble," said Rees.

"Long story be-buggered! This is a colliery! Not a bloody streetmarket! Got talked into it. Soft bugger!" scoffed Tom.

"Are things that bad with you, then?" asked Eric.

"Not me – Richard and Beth. Rich has been out of work now eighteen months. And he can't repay his mortgage – not without my help," Rees tried to explain.

"Do they know what you're doing?" Eric inquired with caution.

"No! Hell's bells, no! Beth would go through the roof!" Rees eased Gwyn's head on his arm. "Like I said I couldn't sell the house. So this was the only way I could think of helping them. You scrimp to put 'em in college – and in 1990 they land up on the dole!"

"Aye, but why the hell didn't you sign on full time?" asked Eric.

"They didn't want me full time. I think they're finding it hard to keep going – power stations buying imported, foreign coal. Dilwyn Jenkins offered me three nights a week. So I took it. Beggars can't be choosers."

"You know if anyone asks: What's the worst thing to happen to the ordinary British in the last thousand years?, It would be a toss-up between the Black Death and Maggie bloody Thatcher!" snarled Tom.

"If you were a politician they'd find you a cushie job abroad," grinned Eric.

"Abroad would do me nicely, right now," said Rees, wryly.

"Treorchy not bad this time of year!" said Tom.

Treorchy'd suit me fine – and old Gwyn by here I expect," said Rees quietly. He looked down at Gwyn. Gwyn's eyes were wide open, looking straight up at him.

"Gwyn! For Christ's sake!" Rees gasped.

"Hey! Gwyn boy!" Eric was around to the other side, his hand on Gwyn's chest. "Gwyn! Gwyn! Come on lad! Gwyn!"

Gwyn's eyes moved from one face to another, his lips moving as if he wanted to speak.

"Gwyn! What's up my old mate?" asked Tom, his voice surprisingly soft. "What's up old lad?"

A look of terror filled Gwyn's eyes, he sighed deeply, his whole body convulsed, his teeth clenched tight. His eyes closed and air escaped between his slightly parted lips.

"He's gone?" whispered Tom.

Eric put the tips of his fingers against Gwyn's throat, smiled with relief, "No!"

"Bloody hell!" muttered Tom. "Never a dull moment."

They huddled together and listened to the reassuring sounds of the rescue team clawing its way towards them. Suddenly, from directly above their heads, there was a terrific crash.

"Jesus Nellie!" Eric leapt away.

Hearts pounding, they listened to stones hurtling down from high up in the chimney of the fall, smashing to smithereens overhead and showering them with flakes of shale and bits of bark from the shattered roof.

The ground around them settled, and there was a surprise bonus. The rescuers suddenly seemed much closer.

Eric was off the mark like a shot. "I'll give 'em a tap! Let 'em know we're OK!"

The buoyant signal rang out, they listened to the steady hammering beyond the outby.

"Hey! I got it!" Eric beamed as he knelt astride the rail. "I got it! How to get you off the hook, Rees! Tell them you were with them," indicating with his thumb to the outby. "The lads will go along with it, guarantee. And you can bet our Mr Jenkins won't be broadcasting the fact that he's employing hobblers!" Eric was elated as he crawled back.

Tom put his arm around Rees's shoulders. "You've cracked it, Eric! This is one place you won't bump into DHSS inspectors – That's for bloody sure! We'll say you're one of the rescuers – we'll say you're a volunteer! Have you mentioned in dispatches yet. Old Murphy would be proud of you!"

"Who's Murphy?" asked Eric, laughing.

"A breed apart," said Tom affectionately. "We both worked as his collier boys. One story he used to tell us was about the time he'd go sheep shearing. When things were slack in the pits.

"On one big farm, same pot of cawl on the stove all week! The cook, a large, not too clean woman, with a fierce temper, slung everything and anything into the pot. Middle of summer, knuckle of ham-bones alive with blow fly maggots, in it went! Nobody'd tell her! All too afraid! But Murphy thought, well at least he'd mention it to her. So up he went for a second helping. Can I have another bowl of your most excellent cawl, Cook – and will you put plenty of that rice in it, if you please?" Tom beamed. The cold, the wet and the terror forgotten.

The morning sky was crystal clear, after a month of constant torrential rain. A reporter was describing the scene to a T.V. camera. In the background was the long drawn-out ringing made by a taut steel hawser, as it tamped off the spinning idlers. The spake, bedecked with the twinkling, white lights of the rescuers, came out of the black mouth of the Drift. The bodies of the three dead miners lay one to a carriage, each wrapped in a grey woollen blanket. The reporter explained, "Two days ago, the rescuers thought they heard faint tapping. Then came another massive fall of roof, injuring two of the rescuers, and sealing the fate of the three men. They are Mr Eric Bowen, aged forty, married with three young children. Mr Tom Pugh, late fifties, married with a grown up family. Mr Rees Lewis, in his sixties, widower, with a married daughter. After four days and five nights of superhuman effort, this harrowing drama, played out in the darkness a mile under a Welsh mountain, has come to an end. This is Jamie Dene at the Camnant Drift Mine, in South West Wales."

He walked over to where some of the rescuers were standing, offering his hand, "Could I have a word? My name's Jamie Dene."

"I know – seen you on T.V.!"

"And you are?"

"Gwyn. Gwyn Jones!"

"You knew the three men, Gwyn?"

"Yes," said Gwyn. He was covered in slurry, and looked worn out. "Yes, I knew them well. We were mates. I was supposed to be with them – but got held up."

"You were lucky, Gwyn!"

"Yes."

"All this rain we've had – could that cause such a massive roof collapse?"

"It wouldn't have helped."

"I believe the men had made something, Gwyn?"

"This!" Gwyn held out his hand. In his palm there was a crude crucifix, made of two fragments of wood bound together by a strand of shiny detonator fuse wire. "They had one each – and this one – laying on a stone near them – to the outby."

The sight of the most brutal of killing devices, that was for so many the sign of faith and hope, caused a dull ache in the pit of Jamie Dene's stomach. "What do you make of it, Gwyn?"

"Don't know.... What do you turn to when the noose is being pulled tight? Lucky charms? This?" Gwyn's voice was quiet with rage: he closed his fist over the small, crudely made crucifix.

THE MAN WHO STAYED
A MINER

"Our grandfathers must have been running away from the police when they came to live in the Banwen," Peggy muttered. She was waiting for the kettle to boil and frowning at the rain being driven sideways, like blades, past the kitchen window.

The back door opened, a gust of wind rushed in and slammed the kitchen door shut. There was the sound of a struggle and the back door was closed.

"Hello! Anybody home?"

The kitchen door opened, a battered pork-pie trilby hat, that looked as if it had been in every gang fight from the Bronx to Chicago, came around the door, topping a face that looked as if it had worn the hat through every one of those fights. Mr Coombes wore a serge overcoat, mauve and faded, buttoned to the neck, with a length of bailing cord pulled tight about the waist as a belt. Cord yorks held the bottoms of his trousers around the tops of his hob-nailed boots. The uncloved fist that held his shopping bag was big enough to fill a good-sized face. But in reality, that fist had never been used for anything more violent than topping and tailing turnips on finger-numbing mornings in the frost-covered fields of Herefordshire. Making and playing violins, or gently setting into splints the torn and broken limbs of his workmates in the darkness of the coal face. Other times just tapping out words, hundreds of thousands of words, on an antiquated typewriter. Words that told of his life, his work, his concern for his friends and their families; or his anger at the wanton cutting down of a chestnut tree. Words that were translated into many languages and sent by book and on the air waves around the world.

"What are you doing out on a morning like this, Mr Coombes? You're soaked!"

"Had to get Mary's prescription, Peg."

"Sit down, I'll make you a cup of coffee – then George can drive you home."

It was because of my wife Peggy that I had got to know Bert Lewis Coombes. Peggy was the local newsagent, Bert called at her shop every week to pay for his papers and pick up the *Writer*. Before the advent of television, the people at the top end of the Dulais Valley were avid readers. Reading what seemed like every title in print. *The John Bull*, for its short stories and free household insurance, *Tit Bits*, *Answers*, *Nursing*, *Mirror*, *Mining*, *Pigeon Fancier*, *Dog World*, *Practical Mechanics*, *Boxing*, *Wireless*, *Picture Post*, *Illustrated News* and even the *Razzel*. But only one customer took the *Writer*. B.L. Coombes.

That singled him out, then finding he had the same beginnings as my own father. Born in the eighteen nineties, starting their hard working lives as fourteen year-old farm boys. Understanding what it meant to be hired out for six pounds for six months, to work from sun up to sun down.

There it was, I suppose: shared tribal values.

Then like very many other migrants to the coalfields of the South Wales valleys, Mr Coombes found work and a pretty wife in Cwm Nedd, where he started and ended his mining career.

Bert and Mary Coombes came to live at Nantyfedwen, a smallholding on the north bank of the Pyrddin, during the Second World War. Unlike most of his workmates, who were second and third generation miners, Bert Coombes still possessed the skills of the countryman. Able to churn butter, press cheese, plait a hawthorn hedge, help a ewe bring a lamb or slit a cockerel's gizzard with one deft, merciful stroke. He took great pride in those primary skills. A competence no doubt that had a lot to do with his particular outlook on life. He had mixed and worked with the famous and the frivolous, but chose always to stay inside his own frontiers. Somewhere in his radio play, *I Stayed a Miner*, there is probably an explanation.

I once remember telling him, that in the 1945 election, the British people had brought about a revolution and had done it without spilling one drop of blood: that was something we should be proud of.

"Let's hope that we all won't live to regret it!" he replied.

His answer surprised me. I had never heard him profess to being a pacifist but had heard him say many times that he was against capital punishment. His favourite story about the Royal Family was to recall the day that King George the sixth and his consort, the present day Queen Mother were progressing down the Neath valley, on their grand tour of Wales. It was a beautiful summer's day and they were still celebrating the coronation.

The Royal cortege had passed Pentreclwyddu, and the lodge where Mary and Bert Coombes lived came into sight. Bert insisted that at that point the Queen tapped the King's arm and pointed out Bert and Mary's flower garden. It was a blaze of colour against the dense green of the forest background. The telling of that story, in the opinion of one of his closest friends and admirers, Doctor Dafydd Aubrey Thomas, put Bert somewhere among the ranks of the tidy left.

But Bert was never slow to lash out at those of the working class who behaved badly. In his *War Diary of a Welsh Miner*, he described as animals the handful of men who stole the possessions of others in the changing rooms of the pithead baths.

And in his much-published short story *Twenty Tons of Coal*, he is acutely aware of the bitter compromises miners had to make. If he tells the truth at the inquest, about the deputy's wilful neglect of duty that had caused the death of his friend, Griff, the dead man's widow and his five children would get nothing. The insurance company would simply claim that the neglect absolved them of liability. But to say nothing would let off the guilty deputy. This constant humiliation that he and others had had to suffer over the years made him very angry, especially with those that didn't do their best to make nationalisation work for the industry and for the country.

Mining in the Thirties was brutal: it made men tough mentally and physically. And it was that toughness that was the mother and father of his strong belief. Bert subscribed to the notion that there are two kinds of working class. Those with *trefn* and those without, and it was the paramount duty of the former to help the latter up off their knees.

Bert finished his coffee: the rain had eased and we set off for Nantyfedwen. I turned the car where the Sarn Helen (the Roman Road) leaves the Caer (fort) and goes on to Brecon and Chester.

Bert Coombes had a droll sense of humour. We would sit and look at the bare, bleak campsite. The grass scorched to a crisp pale yellow by the raw wind. We would wonder about the young men who would have been sent to garrison this outpost of the Roman Empire, almost two thousand years before. And imagined the possible reactions of a young Roman soldier, walking up from a sun drenched beach, perhaps in the south of France; and his comrades gleefully waiting to tell him.

"Your name's up on part one orders."

"What for?"

"You've been posted."

"Posted! To where?"

"Banwen!"

And decided that it could have been thinking along those lines that brought the scholar, Sir Mortimer Wheeler to the conclusion on which he based his supposition that the band of Roman deserters, the original "Dirty Dozen", who for a time terrorised this part of Wales were deserters from this very Fort. In those days it most surely must have been a place to run away from.

The publisher Gollancz once said of him, "He's the only writer able to write about the plight of the working class and not become hysterical." At that time, in the mid Thirties, seven hundred and fifty thousand men worked in Britain's coalmines and Bert Coombes was one of them. Part of a unique community of men, women and children, perhaps numbering as many as four million people in all. Living out their lives in hundreds of mining villages across the length and breadth of the land. Each village as beholden to its mine as a crew is to its ship.

Bert Coombes's vivid descriptions of life at the coalface were the real thing. The to and fro of village life within the constant sound of the winding engine. The commonplace task of laying out the young dead and returning the stretcher, scrubbed spotlessly clean to the first-aid room, illustrated clearly the way of life of the British coal-mining families.

Always at the hub of Britain's mighty industrial engine, migrating from one coalfield to another to harvest a crop that had ripened in the sun three hundred and twenty million years before, and always tenaciously hanging on to the rural values of their beginnings.

A coalmine acquires a character of its own. Never still, always shifting, creaking, filling up with water. Sometimes behaving badly and frightening the life out of everybody. Other times lining pockets with gold. Coombes's competent and faithful portrayal of this unparalleled, extraordinary community, sadly now wiped out to satisfy political dogma, must surely be down to the fact that he stayed a miner.

Later, when I had retired, like Bert I walked the Roman road and like Bert, I was minus a few pieces. Bert had walked on the Sarn Helen every day and he had said that simply having his feet on that ancient highway inspired him. He gloried in the work ethic of those soldier-engineers. He had shovelled and split rocks, been wet through, and sometimes felt like death with the 'flu. So he reckoned he had a good idea of how those lads must have felt, building those great earth and clay ramparts at the fort across the stream from his home.

Bert spent the last thirty years of his life at Nantyfedwen Farm. A violinist, violin maker, farmer, coalminer, unionist, pamphleteer, and story-teller. Who would not, at any price, have a straight path anywhere in his garden. The squat, square figure of B.L. Coombes seemed to fit comfortably and easily into the fabled land of the Banwen Pyrddin.

LOVE AND WAR

"**Y**ou're off to Maymyo."

"Where the hell's Maymyo?"

"Christ knows! But that's where you're going. And by train."

"Train?"

"Yes, ten of you. Some R.E.'s, and some Ox and Bucks. It'll give the civilians on the train a bit of confidence. Dacoits took some pot shots at the last one."

"Nice! How long are we gone for?"

"It'll take three or four days to get there. The track's not that clever. Then bring a train back. It was an old hill station. You'll have ten days there, out of this heat for a bit. That's all the jen, as far as I know, OK!"

Rangoon General Railway Station was showing signs of neglect: it was tidy but threadbare, like the Anglo-Indians that ran it. The train was made up and standing in the station but the engine had not been coupled. There were five carriages, painted a flat brown, barred windows without class, and a brake-van with an observation platform. The Regimental Train Officer came over.

"You lot in the last carriage with half the R.E.'s. The Ox and Bucks in the first carriage with the rest of the engineers. Your rations are on the train. But every man must see to his own drinking water. There's a water bowzer in the brake van. Right?"

Five men to a compartment, the way they had crossed India eighteen months ago. The pulsating afternoon heat bounced up off the flagstoned platform. It was a relief to take their webbing off.

The backs of the seats lifted up to make the two middle bunks, the luggage racks made two, and the seats made the other two. Their rifles and bandoleers went on the deck, under the seats for safe keeping. They had two water bottles a man – one tin,

British army issue and one skin, Indian army issue – that they tied to the window bars to keep cool. They slung bed-rolls and the rest of their kit up onto the spare luggage rack, where their K rations were stacked.

There was a bump as the engine was shunted and coupled up. Slowly they moved away and a warm breeze wafted in through the window.

"Char cahna sahib ?"

The sound of the char wallah making his way along the train had five dark green, enamelled mugs at the ready. Their K rations: two packs a day for each man. Breakfast, one small round tin filled with two mouthfuls of spongy scrambled egg and bits of bacon. A bar of prunes or apricots, a bar of hard chocolate. Hard tack biscuits, baked and re-baked to give them a shelf-life of at least sixty years, and able to shatter most sets of teeth in one bite. The dinner pack was the same except for the contents of the tin, which would be Spam or Spam and dried egg. The hot char was ideal for soaking the biscuits in: just dunking was futile.

Taff climbed onto the top bunk and looked out through the vents above the window. They were going quite slow, in a curve. In the late afternoon light he could see the magnificent spire of the Swadagon pagoda, covered in twenty two carat gold leaf. Someone had said it was eighty feet higher than St. Paul's. In the clear dark-blue afternoon sky its slender curve reached up into a fine, round, golden canopy where the gentle spirit of Buddha was supposed to rest.

The train stopped at Pegu. He bought some sweet-limes, a coconut, a mango and a mug of char. They had covered about fifty miles and it was dark. Sentries were posted. Pegu was a small town, mostly shacks. The war was over, but seventy murders had been reported in the area in the last month. They took water, coal and a few passengers, then slowly clattered away to the north.

By morning they were on the wide Pegu plain with green paddy fields stretching to the horizon on either side. Farmers working in the fields lifted their heads from their work and waved, no doubt glad to see the chuffing, puffing sign of normality return.

After months in the Delta, where the limit of the horizon was the far bank perhaps a hundreds yard away, it was an experience to be moving at a slow but steady pace across the great plain. The Pegu Yoma gave Burma its distinctive fame, as the Rice Bowl of Asia. The rice was still growing. It had not yet taken up all the water in the paddies and was still green. A vibrant living, growing green, streaked with silver strips of sun-bright water. He was glad he had copped for this detail.

The far away hills to the east held a darker part of Britain's past: the Opium Triangle. For fifty years the British were the biggest drug pushers in the world, and squaddies like him guarded the golden loot.

The char wallah had cornered the market on the train. He gathered up their empty water bottles, filled them from the bowser and hung them back on the window bars.

"Dhobi sahib?" He was the laundry man too.

The last two compartments of their carriage held the ablution block. One for washing and dobbing, the other lavatories. These were three holes cut in the floor, with checkerplate foot blocks and a handrail, so that you wouldn't be thrown forward on your head, or backwards on your arse if the train came to a sudden stop.

The wash basins were a teak trough divided into five separate compartments. The water flushed down from a large tank and was controlled by wooden plugs which acted as taps. The water drained down into another trough and then out through the side of the carriage.

They made a short stop at a small place called Pyu. The peddlars were noticeably cleaner than their city brothers. He bought some sliced pineapple and some more sweet-limes.

Taff was on stand-to with Turner. This involved sitting in the corridor for the day; Lee-Enfield, magazine charged, safety catch on, cotton bandoleer, while occasionally taking a dekho along the train. Children stopped their play and ran towards the train. The soldiers waved to them as they slowly got smaller and smaller until they became tiny specks.

It was late afternoon when they arrived in Toungoo on the second day. They had covered a third of the way. Some passengers got off. Two women got on. The R.E.'s drained the drinking water bowser into the wash-tank, then refilled it with fresh water. The engine that had been uncoupled returned from the siding, water-tank and coal-tank full.

For a while the track ran parallel with the Sittang river that flowed to the Gulf of Martaban hundreds of miles to the south. He ate his dinner sitting in the corridor: a tin of spam, a bar of dried apricots, chocolate and a sweet-lime washed down with a mug of sweet char.

In the late-afternoon they were stood down. Taff unloaded his rifle, pushed it back under the bottom bunk with his bandolier, and climbed onto his bed. He slept like a nineteen year old boy. In the morning he woke and looked through the vents into the clear shining air that had rolled down off the Shan Hills. He believed he could taste it and understood what people meant when they spoke of the nectar of the Gods.

The train was moving faster now, the track was in much better condition. Pyinmsna flipped past: they had reached the Meiktila plain. A few months earlier the plain had been a place where violent death had pervaded every ditch, every clump of trees, every broken building. Soldiers had stabbed, hacked and blasted each other at arms length and had heard that last rasp of wind escape from their dying enemy. A cruel place. Now, nourished by the warm monsoon rains it had clothed itself in a lush, luxurious living green.

They were making good time; by mid-day they were pulling in to Yamethin. It was a bustling place, the platform was crowded. Taff looked at the people surging onto the train. The three carriages allotted to civilian passengers were going to be packed if they all got on board. But half the people on the platform had come to see the other half off.

A young woman was selling piping hot rice; it looked very appetising. He looked at her hands as she offered the rice. They were spotlessly clean. He shouted to Turner to pass the mess–tins out. He bought two portions, one for him and one for Turner.

He enjoyed the rice and sat looking out to the west. The forest stretched way to the horizon and rising from it, like discarded stage sets, were abandoned pagodas, garlanded with vines. Treasures left by the Mons, the great scholars of Burma. A dynasty of architects who went on to teach the Khmers who in turn built the great temples of Angkor in Indo–China.

His life had changed. It could have been yesterday he was working on the coal face. And hoping, always hoping to try for a bit of awkward necking on the back seats of the cinema. It was embarrassing to think of, even at this distance. Now most of the lads had been to a brothel or at least claimed they'd been. One or two had picked up a dose. Perhaps more than just one or two. He winced at the stories. It was even claimed that a Tory MP wanted men returning from Burma to wear a yellow arm band.

Smith had persuaded Turner, Jock and himself to go to a brothel on Christmas Eve.

"Only B.O.R.'s, definitely ! Word of 'oner!" he had claimed.

Smith was a twenty year-old cockney who knew it all. The brothel was in the out-of-bounds part of the city. The stench in the narrow streets cut through him, but they pressed on under Smith's encouragement.

"In ere."

They climbed a darkened narrow stairs onto the first floor. A single low wattage bulb hung from the ceiling, showing a room partitioned off into small, low sections with hessian sacking. The Indian brothel keeper was all smiles, and assured them that the bibbies would be brought directly. Two girls came in from the next room. It was hard to tell their age: their faces, except for their lips, eyes and neck were painted completely white. In the hard light of the single electric light bulb, he had the sensation of standing in an open grave. The hessian cubicles made his skin crawl. But worse were the dark sad eyes of the girls, framed by the white masks.

"I'm buggering off!"

"Taff, for Christ sake!" Smith protested.

He made for the stairs. Turner followed.

"Piss off then!" Smith's curse came after them.

As they burst into the street they heard the sound of army boots.

"Red caps!" They scrambled behind a pile of refuse. The smell of rotting cabbage filled his nostrils. But it wasn't Red caps. It was three African Rifles who went straight into the doorway of the brothel. So much for Smith and his bloody British Other Ranks only.

The rumours claimed that if you picked up a dose of the African strain, the end of it would drop off. For nine days Smith and Jock lived in sheer terror, afraid even to shake the droppers off. He smiled remorsefully, uneasy with the memory. It would have been better if things had been different.

They were still making good time; Kyankse, just south of Mandalay by morning. At Mandalay they put a loco at each end. The train set out heading north-east, towards southwest China. The climb started almost right away, on the steepest gradient he had ever seen. Both engines, one pushing, one pulling were making a terrific noise, sending steam and smoke billowing in every direction. The train was at such an acute angle that anything not fastened down began to roll along the floor.

The track was bordered on one side by a sheer cliff while on the other the rock fell away to space. Then it levelled off as they slowed down and eased into a dead–end.

The points were changed at the far end of the train, the throttle opened, the wheels spun, then gripped, driving the train up in the opposite direction. They were climbing the Shan hills by way of a track cut diagonally into the cliff face. First going from west to east, into a dead-end shunt, then from east to west and so on, to seven thousand feet. The air was thin and the view like nothing he or the other lads had ever seen. To the north, the grey blue ridges of Nyenchentangla ranges, and the mighty Mount Minya Konka, 24,309 feet high. And somewhere in the distance the source of two of the greatest rivers in the world, the Salween and the Irrawady. There had been some rough old times over the last two years but this made up for it.

When they got off the train at Maymyo it was late afternoon. Four trucks waited, ready to take them to their billets. Their truck pulled up outside a large red brick house, built in Tudor style, with a well kept, beautiful garden. It didn't feel real: it could have been Surrey. Coolies carried their kit into the house and up to their rooms. There were five bedrooms, two to a room. He shared with Turner. Downstairs there was a kitchen, mess room, and a sitting-room with a card table. The rest of the downstairs was taken over by the cook, the bobagy, his wife. There was also the pantry and a large bathroom with five showers and for the first time in two years, WC's.

They went down for their evening meal. Soup, roast mutton, sweet potato, greens, gravy. For sweet, sliced banana and mango. They ate in absolute silence. The house dhobi wallah collected their dirty clothes. He looked at the soldiers: "Cahna jute sahib?" He pointed to his feet. He was offering them new shoes.

Taff enjoyed a bargain. 'Kitna rupee?'

"Pac rupee, sahib"

"Car ?"

"Ok, sahid. Car rupee!"

He measured their feet, with a slide measure they had not seen since their school days back in the Thirties.

After four nights being rocked to and fro on the train it was a treat to lie on a bed that was still. Outside there was some sound, a few crickets, and the screech of an owl, but nothing like the din that accompanied the coming of night in the delta. And it was cool.

He woke in the morning feeling better than he'd felt for ages. Breakfast was porridge, delicious tinned American bacon, eggs, tomatoes and fried bread.

The men dressed. They were ready to go out and give the town the once over.

"You wearing your ribbons?" asked Turner.

"Aye! Why not!"

They had been awarded their ribbons two weeks ago, but had never worn them. The 1939-45 Star and the Burma Star. The ribbons were really just a brooch but they added status and a little colour to their jungle green bush shirts.

The house in which they were billeted was surrounded by an ornamental park with well-tended flower beds and flourishing shrubs. Other houses, replicas of England, filled the hillside, separated by acres of well-mown grass. This was Bara Sahib country.

Two horse drawn garries came to a stop by the front door, offering them a lift into the town.

"Maymo jaiga, sahib?"

They got in, five in each, it should have been four, but it was a short ride and on the flat.

Maymyo was neat and clean, the shops laid out very much like back home, but the contents and use in some of them were very different. Tattooing: three shops in a row. Shops selling teak and ivory carving. Shoe shops that would make you a pair of shoes in one hour. Tailors cutting a suit in less. Goldsmiths, ready to set blood-red Burmese rubies into the jewellery of your choice. Barber's, photographers.

Barber's first, photographers second, with medal ribbons worn. Make a bit of an impression back home. There was a dance hall: admission one rupee, then four annas a dance. With a bar and restaurant.

Taff walked back with Turner to the house, ready to take a

shower after the haircut. Afterwards they lounged around, reading old magazines. *Country Life, The Tatler,* the names tried to affirm something. He thought of the people who had bought them, enjoying his subtle theft.

The cook had prepared them a chicken dinner, with spotted dick for afters. They had seen a gymkhana advertised in town but had no idea what it was. On the poster there were drawings of horses jumping. Back home they'd had horse shows. Best turned out colliery horse, Galloway's, musical chairs and hurdles. But it was just called the show, and the whole valley turned up.

When they got to the gymkhana Taff realised this was another kind of show. There were cavalry horses sixteen or seventeen hands high and big Arizonian mules. He felt the label on a camp coffee bottle had come to life. Resplendent in their white and scarlet uniforms, the governor's bodyguard stood sentinel outside his tent. Servants in snow-white uniforms, but without shoes, scurried about. It was as if the war had never happened.

They were preparing for a mule race. The Indian muleteers were tough and enjoyed living up to their motto: *If you come to a mountain the mule can't climb, carry the baggage to the top of the mountain, then come back down and carry the mule.* The race was to be run with no saddles or bridles, just a rope halter: about fifteen mules lined up for the two circuits. The speed with which the long-legged mules moved, surprised the soldiers. They were used to seeing the hard-working, patient, cross–breeds picking their way slowly up steep mountain paths. The animals brought the crowd to its feet. One rider, trying to show off, rode at full speed with both hands above his head, then right opposite the governor's tent his mule stopped dead, its front legs rigged. The rider took off vertically, getting the biggest cheer of the day.

When the soldiers got back to the house, their new shoes had been delivered. Calf hide shoes, hand made, perfect fit, for four rupees. In English money six shillings.

They showered again, put on their newly laundered uniforms, new shoes and set off for the dance. The price had gone up, it was now eight annas a dance. Taff wasn't very good at dancing, he wished that he'd paid more attention at the local YMCA dances. He gave the cashier three rupees; admission and four dances. He'd see how he got on after that. At the bar they had local hooch and some American canned beer at a rupee a can, expensive, but better than risking the local stuff. Not that he or any of them drank much on a British soldier's pay.

The dance-hall was clean and decorated with what someone had thought was good taste. Some of the Ox and Bucks were there, he lifted his hand in acknowledgement. The beer tasted like nothing. The band started to play: Red Sails in the Sunset. One or two of the lads walked over to the girls, the dance hostesses. They were a mixture of Chinese and Burmese, all pretty girls. The Chinese dressed in their long tight fitting dresses, split at the bottom, to just above the knee. The Burmese in their brightly coloured longees and white lace bodices. The girls all had jet black hair which they wore pulled back into a bun. He was relieved to see there were no Fred Astaire's on the floor, one or two were even worse than him.

It was her perfume he was aware of first: a delicious, delicate fragrance. A scent that could only belong to this place. She was smiling down at him, she was about seventeen, she was perfect. "You dance Johnie?"

Taff muttered, "yes", and stood up. He fumbled in his pocket for the ticket to give her. She put her hand in his, it was three long years since he'd held a girls hand. It was small and soft. He turned to face her and they just shuffled around the floor. The music stopped, he felt a flutter of panic. What if one of those ugly bastards came over and asked her to dance? He didn't want to get into a fight, but he would if he had to.

"Drink?", he motioned with his hand. She grinned at him, he knew she understood him. He motioned again, "What?'

"Mango, please?"

He sat her down in his chair. He pointed to his friend

Turner, "Turner." then pointed to himself "Me Taff!"

Turner winked at him.

"Can I get you one, Turn?" Turner shook his head. He came back with the cool mango juice for her. He pulled up a chair and as he sat down touched her hand, "Your, name?"

"Mai!", she laughed.

A good-looking Chinese woman in her twenties walked on and stood behind the microphone. The band started playing Blue Moon: the singer had a lovely contralto voice. Mai touched his arm: they got up to dance. She was working: he'd have to pay attention; if she sat down someone else would take her to dance.

He planned it out: he'd buy Turner's four tickets off him – that would sort the first part of the night.

She was standing closer to him now as they moved around the floor, his right hand was on her waist. She was small, but strong; he could feel the fine firm body under the satin of her longee. With her left hand she touched his hair, said something and giggled. In the two years he'd been in Burma his hair had been bleached in the sun to the colour of straw. The local people found it strange, all of them having the same black hair. He'd be twenty in a month, and this was the best day of his life. Turner's tickets took them to the interval.

They walked out into the garden and over to a viewing point. A young Burmese man called to her, she waved a reply.

He rested his elbows on the wall and looked out at the moonlit mountains, the highest peaks capped with snow. The moon was suspended in a clear sky like a huge silver plate. He looked at her and remembered the name of the girl in the film, *Lost Horizon*, the ageless girl in Shangri-la, Lo-Tsen and Conway describing her, "She's like a little ivory doll." She looked at him. She was exquisite. He felt the soft, velvet tips of her fingers on the bare skin of his arm.

A rifle shot rang out, it startled a hawk and echoed in the valley below. He didn't hear it, but through a red haze, he had the sensation that his pockets were being emptied. All she wanted was for him and his like, with all their vulgar paraphernalia, to be out of her country.

When they caught her they would hang her.

Reviews for *Boys of Gold*

'The real gamble for any writer of our bright new millennium is to write with sentiment and feeling...Thus I was refreshed and encouraged, in reading George Brinley Evan's *Boys of Gold*, to encounter a writer who is prepared to take this risk.... The book exudes a memorable sense of decency and compassion.'

Robert Nisbet   *Planet*

'Sudden and violent death is not confined to war as Evans represents the precarious working lives of miners in stories that demand re-reading.'

The New Welsh Review

'In the seven brief, lyrical sketches that make up *Boys of Gold*, George Evans moves between the perilous coal mines and idyllic countryside of Wales and the jungles and whorehouses of Burma. The contrast between beautiful landscapes and the harsh conditions they conceal is what's most striking.'

Publishers Weekly

'Told through seven short stories, Evans opens with a shocking account of the thoughts and fears of a young soldier, fighting for king and country while remembering the idyllic lifestyle of his rural upbringing. His tale shifts from war to mining, the two elements he writes about with confidence and conviction.

The Western Mail